This book
belongs to

_____

# EGMONT
*We bring stories to life*

First published in Great Britain 2008
by Egmont UK Limited
239 Kensington High Street, London W8 6SA
BARBIE and associated trademarks and trade dress are owned by,
and used under licence from, Mattel, Inc.
© 2008, Mattel, Inc.

ISBN 978 1 4052 4197 7

1 3 5 7 9 10 8 6 4 2

Printed in China

# The Story Book

EGMONT

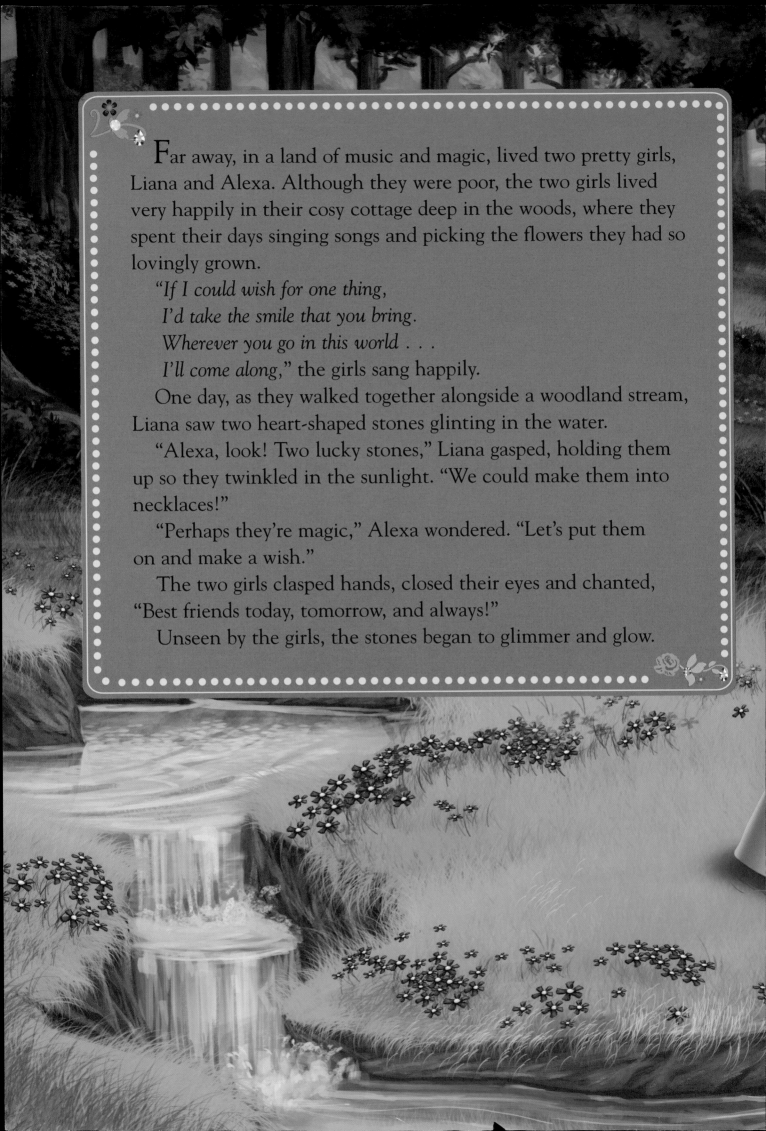

Far away, in a land of music and magic, lived two pretty girls, Liana and Alexa. Although they were poor, the two girls lived very happily in their cosy cottage deep in the woods, where they spent their days singing songs and picking the flowers they had so lovingly grown.

*"If I could wish for one thing,*
*I'd take the smile that you bring.*
*Wherever you go in this world . . .*
*I'll come along,"* the girls sang happily.

One day, as they walked together alongside a woodland stream, Liana saw two heart-shaped stones glinting in the water.

"Alexa, look! Two lucky stones," Liana gasped, holding them up so they twinkled in the sunlight. "We could make them into necklaces!"

"Perhaps they're magic," Alexa wondered. "Let's put them on and make a wish."

The two girls clasped hands, closed their eyes and chanted, "Best friends today, tomorrow, and always!"

Unseen by the girls, the stones began to glimmer and glow.

The next day, the girls were carrying flowers to the market when they saw a poor old woman by the side of the road. The girls shared their lunch with her and, in return, she gave them an old hand mirror from her bag of treasures.

Back home, Liana and Alexa polished the mirror until it gleamed, singing as they worked. Suddenly, another voice joined in with their song. A beautiful girl was singing from inside the glass! Her name was Melody.

Melody told the friends that she used to live in the Diamond Castle, the home of music, as the apprentice to three Muses – Lydia, Dori and Phedra. "Lydia wanted the Diamond Castle to herself," said Melody. "The Muses gave me the key to the castle, and tried to reason with Lydia. But she turned them to stone with her evil flute, and sent her winged serpent after me. I fled. When I saw the old woman by the roadside, I blew my magic whistle and hid inside her mirror. But the whistle broke. I'm trapped forever!"

In a dark cavern far away, the evil Muse Lydia was singing an eerie song. In the corner, her pet serpent snorted loudly in his sleep. Suddenly his tongue quivered like a tuning fork. He opened one yellow eye and smirked wickedly.

"Mistress!" he hissed. "The apprentice is alive! I sense her singing, somewhere nearby!"

"Ha! Melody!" sneered Lydia. "Slyder, what are you waiting for? Bring her to me!"

Later, Slyder flew back to the cave, and dropped the old woman at Lydia's feet. "That's not Melody!" scowled Lydia.

"Perhaps she knows where Melody is?" the serpent cringed.

Lydia played a few chilling notes on her snake-like flute. The old woman fell under her spell, and told Lydia dreamily that she had given her mirror to two girls the day before.

"Slyder, find those girls and bring me the mirror!" said Lydia. "Melody must have used her magic to hide in it!"

Liana and Alexa had promised to return Melody to the Diamond Castle and were already trekking along the forest path that led to the castle. They held up the mirror so Melody could show them the way. Soon they came to the Valley of Flowers.

A hollow log rolled down the grassy slope behind them, and to their surprise, out jumped an adorable puppy . . . and then another! Liana named hers Sparkles because of its sparkling eyes, and Alexa named hers Lily.

Later that day, they arrived at a village inn, where the innkeeper told them that his musicians had not turned up. Feeling hungry, Liana and Alexa offered to sing for their supper. But as they began to impress the audience with their song, the hired musicians, identical twins Jeremy and Ian, arrived.

Ian and Jeremy began to charm the girls with their music – little knowing that all the music-making had caught Slyder's attention, and that he and Lydia were drawing near.

Alexa and Liana left the inn, and crept through the dark forest in the moonlight.

Suddenly, Sparkles gave a whine, as Slyder and Lydia swooped down, blocking the girls' way.

"Lydia!" gasped Alexa.

"So you know my name?" asked Lydia with a wicked smile. "I wonder who could have told you! Now give me the mirror," she snapped. But the girls would not give up Melody.

Lydia pulled out her serpent flute. But as her ghostly piping weaved around the girls, she noticed their heart-stone necklaces glimmering magically, protecting them from her evil spell. Liana grabbed Alexa's hand and they dashed through the forest, with Slyder diving clumsily after them.

Just as they grew weary, Liana and Alexa ran into the path of two men on horseback. It was the twins! Jeremy helped Liana on to his horse, Ian took Alexa, and they galloped to safety.

The girls introduced the twins to Melody, and explained that they were on their way to save the Diamond Castle from Lydia. Jeremy and Ian agreed to join them on their journey.

They reached a rushing river. "We just have to make it across to the Seven Stones," said Melody. But before they could work out how to cross, Sparkles and Lily ran behind a boulder to play.

A troll appeared from behind the rock, dangling the poor puppies before the girls. "Looking for these?" he snarled.

Then the troll saw Jeremy and Ian. "You're double trouble!" he roared, dropping the puppies and pulling out a sword. He stabbed the ground by his feet. It crumbled, and the twins fell into a deep pit!

"Answer my riddle," said the troll to the girls, "and you can cross my bridge! What instrument can you hear but can't see or touch?"

Liana and Alexa answered straight away, "Your voice!"

A golden bridge appeared, and they crossed it as the twins crept out of the pit. "Meet you at the Seven Stones!" the boys cried.

Liana, Alexa and the puppies arrived at a beautiful mansion. Alexa knocked on the door. A butler and a maid led them into a hall with a grand table covered in delicious food, all for them!

After tea, the girls explored the house, opening wardrobes and trying on the glistening gowns inside. But Liana soon remembered they were supposed to be taking Melody home.

Melody told the girls not to worry about her. "Just hide me somewhere Lydia can't find me," said the young apprentice.

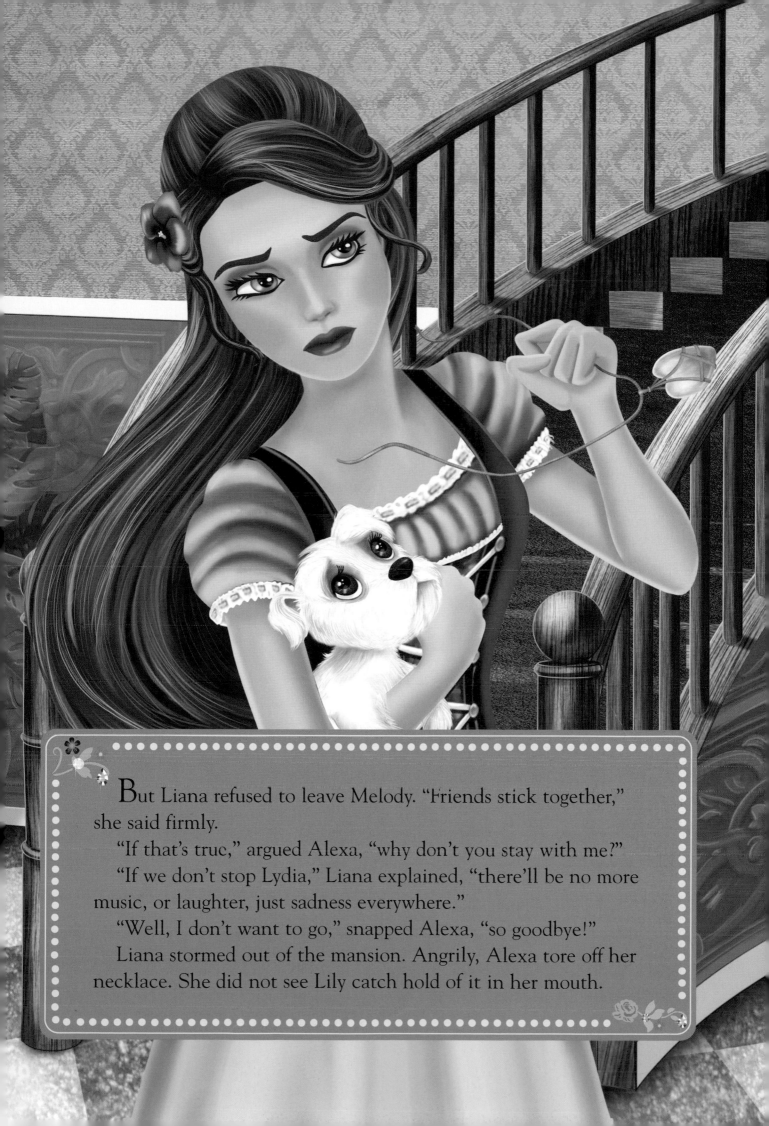

But Liana refused to leave Melody. "Friends stick together," she said firmly.

"If that's true," argued Alexa, "why don't you stay with me?"

"If we don't stop Lydia," Liana explained, "there'll be no more music, or laughter, just sadness everywhere."

"Well, I don't want to go," snapped Alexa, "so goodbye!"

Liana stormed out of the mansion. Angrily, Alexa tore off her necklace. She did not see Lily catch hold of it in her mouth.

That evening, there was a noise at the mansion door. Sure that Liana had come back to apologise, Alexa rushed to open it, but jumped back in fright when she saw Slyder's yellow eyes glinting in the shadows.

Lydia stepped into the room. "Like the mansion, did you?" the evil Muse smiled cruelly. "It was just my way of tricking you! Now give me the mirror!"

Slyder hunted for Melody, while Lydia blew her serpent flute. Without her heart necklace, Alexa was under Lydia's spell, and she sleepily told Lydia where Liana and Melody had gone . . .

Meanwhile, Liana and Sparkles had reached the Seven Stones. As the moon moved out of the shadows to touch them with its silvery light, Liana held Melody up to see. "We're nearly there!" Melody sang happily. "Just down there is the Misty Glade, and the Diamond Castle . . ."

"I wish Alexa was here with us," whispered Liana sadly.

Suddenly, Sparkles barked a warning. But it was too late! Slyder swooped down and scooped Liana up in his claws!

Slyder dropped Liana on to the cold stone floor of Lydia's cavern. "Mistress! I came as fast as I could!"

"You have done well, my pet! Welcome to my lair," Lydia said to Liana, as she tied the young girl's hands behind a pillar. "Alexa told me where to find you. So much for best friends!"

Liana watched in horror as a spellbound Alexa walked to the evil Muse's side. "Alexa!" Liana cried. "Wake up!"

But Alexa listened only to Lydia now.

Lydia snatched the mirror from Liana's basket. "Melody, come out now!" But Melody was hiding. Lydia saw only herself in the reflection.

Furious, she pushed Alexa towards a high ledge. Alexa sleepwalked towards the hissing lava, as Lily tugged at her skirt to wake her. Suddenly, Melody cried, "Stop her, Lydia, please! I'll give you the key to the Diamond Castle." Slyder released Liana but knocked both girls over the ledge with his long, sharp tail!

Luckily, the girls landed safely on a rock shelf, out of Slyder's sight. Liana immediately went to help Alexa, who was still under Lydia's spell. On the ledge above them, Lily was dangling Alexa's necklace, which would surely save her. "Drop, Lily!" Liana shouted, and the little puppy let go of the trinket. Liana caught the necklace, and slipped it over Alexa's neck. "Best friends today, tomorrow, and always," she chanted. Her stone began to glimmer, and magic shot from Alexa's necklace!

Alexa was surrounded by a magic glow and, slowly, she awoke to see the lava all around her. "Liana, where are we?" she gasped.

"In trouble," Liana said with a small smile. "We're in Lydia's cavern. Lydia has Melody – they're on their way to the Diamond Castle!"

"We have to stop them," said Alexa. Sticking closely together, the two friends climbed to the top of the cliff.

The twins arrived at the Seven Stones, but could see no sign of the girls. "They must have gone on without us," said Ian.

Just then, they heard barking, and Sparkles hurtled out of the bushes and yapped loudly at Jeremy. Realising Liana and Alexa must be in trouble, the twins followed the puppy, who led them to where Lily was waiting with the girls!

"We must hurry," said Liana. "Once Lydia finds the castle, nobody will be able to stop her!"

Lydia and Slyder were flying towards the Diamond Castle. Lydia tapped the serpent's snout, and Slyder landed in a moonlit glade with a misty pool. Lydia shook the mirror.

"Where is the castle, Melody? Show it to me, now!" she said.

"It is here, never fear," tinkled Melody.

"You'd better give me the key or I'll throw you in the pool and you'll never see your friends again!" Lydia threatened. Then she stared in shock as Liana and Alexa ran into the glade.

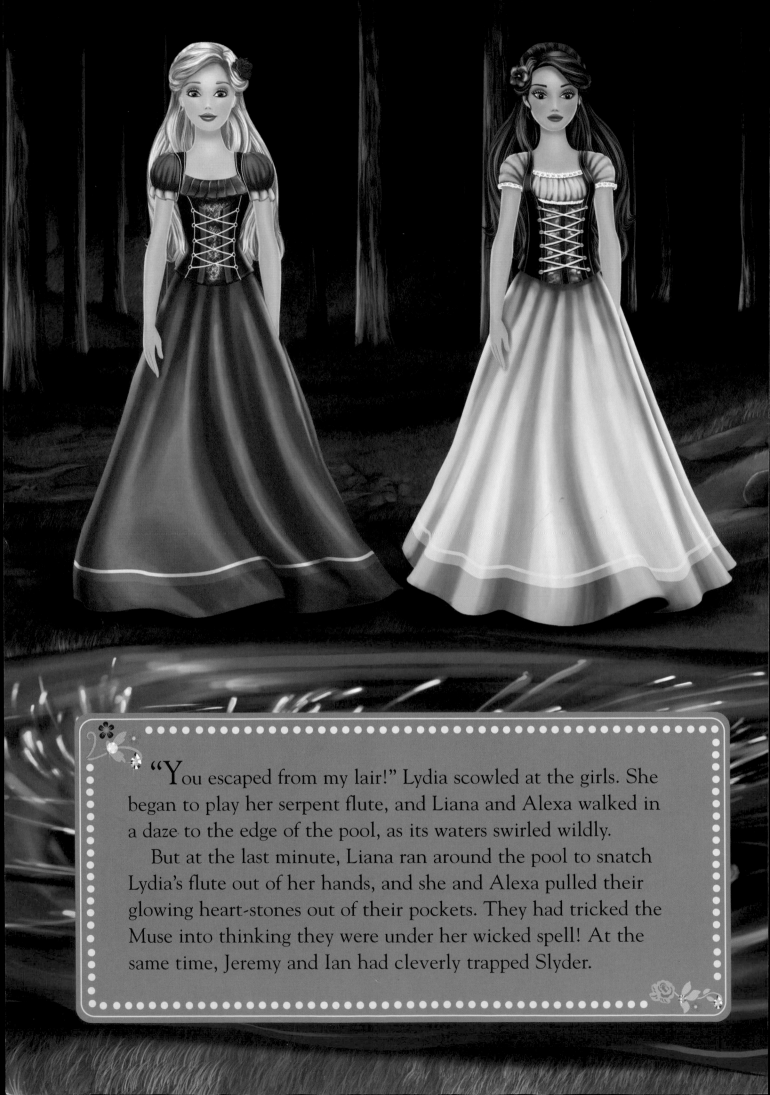

"You escaped from my lair!" Lydia scowled at the girls. She began to play her serpent flute, and Liana and Alexa walked in a daze to the edge of the pool, as its waters swirled wildly.

But at the last minute, Liana ran around the pool to snatch Lydia's flute out of her hands, and she and Alexa pulled their glowing heart-stones out of their pockets. They had tricked the Muse into thinking they were under her wicked spell! At the same time, Jeremy and Ian had cleverly trapped Slyder.

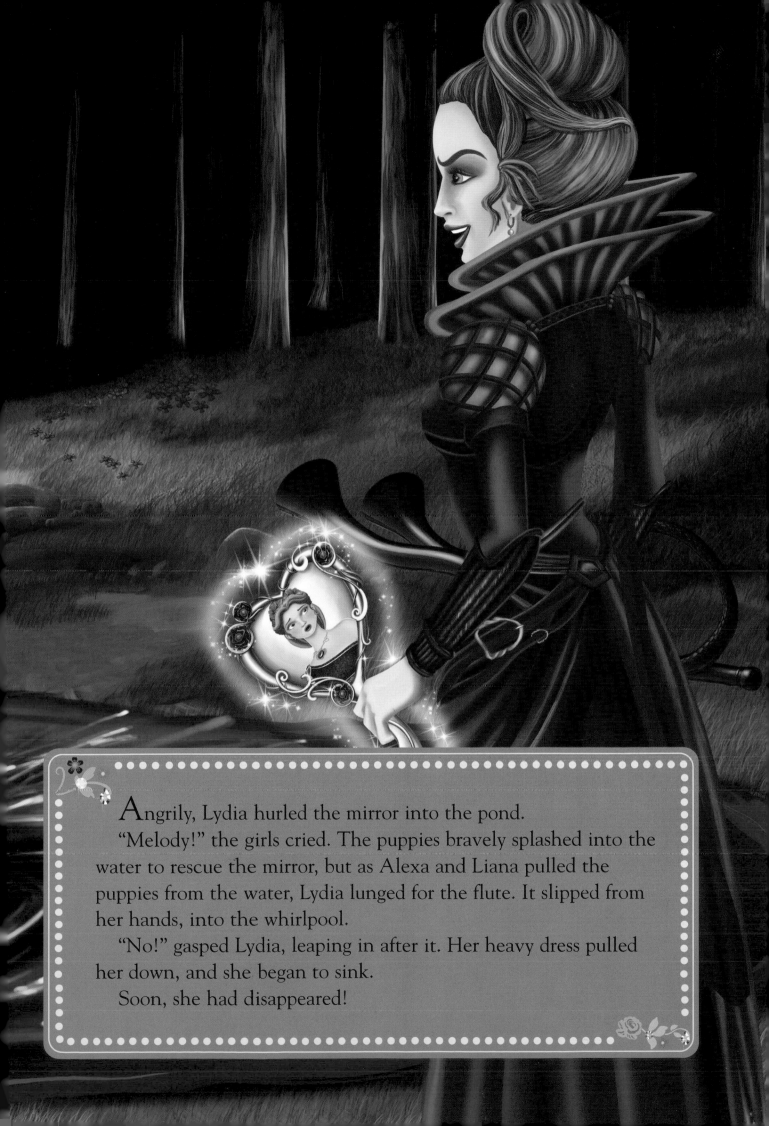

Angrily, Lydia hurled the mirror into the pond.

"Melody!" the girls cried. The puppies bravely splashed into the water to rescue the mirror, but as Alexa and Liana pulled the puppies from the water, Lydia lunged for the flute. It slipped from her hands, into the whirlpool.

"No!" gasped Lydia, leaping in after it. Her heavy dress pulled her down, and she began to sink.

Soon, she had disappeared!

"It's over," breathed Alexa, holding up the mirror to tell Melody. But the glass had cracked when Lydia threw the mirror into the whirlpool. Melody had gone.

Then Alexa had an idea. She and Liana began to sing Melody's favourite song. Suddenly, the Diamond Castle rose up before them, its spires glistening and the sun making a rainbow bridge across the water. In delight, the girls crossed the bridge with Jeremy and Ian not far behind. Then, magically, as they entered the castle gates, Melody burst out of the mirror – free at last!

But their happiness did not last long. With a flap of his wings, in flew Slyder, with an angry, wet Lydia on his back.

Quick as a flash, the girls found the instruments that the Muses had left behind, and began to play a beautiful, magical tune that pulled Lydia's flute from her hand and turned it on her. The evil magic turned Slyder and Lydia to stone!

The Muses, Dori and Phedra, came out of their stony trance and flew into the castle. Delighted that Lydia had been defeated, they crowned Liana and Alexa Princesses of Music!

Dori turned to Melody. "You have proven your worth," she told the young apprentice. "You now replace Lydia as the third Muse!"

The grateful Muses presented Liana and Alexa with jewels to decorate their cottage, some beautiful, musical flowers to plant in their lavish garden and a diamond carriage to take them home.

"Goodbye!" the girls cried, their heart-stones glowing brightly. Best friends today, tomorrow, and always.